SOFIA AND THE MAGICAL BAKERY

BY

Francesca Baldino

SOFIA AND THE MAGICAL BAKERY

Copyright 2024 © Francesca Baldino
All rights reserved.
ISBN:
978-1-966373-34-6
978-1-966373-35-3
978-1-966373-36-0

Published by: SHERO Publishing
Layout & Editing: SHERO Publishing
Illustrations: Camryn Green- CamrynsCreations.com
Book Cover Design- SHERO Publishing

SHERO Publishing
getpublished@sheropublishing.com

For my daughter Sofia,
I hope that you always find
the magic within your soul.
I love you.

SOFIA AND THE MAGICAL BAKERY

3

Once upon a time in the cozy town of Sweetsville, there lived a cheerful girl named Sofia. She had a big heart and an even bigger love for baking.

Every morning, Sofia would rise with the sun, ready to mix flour, sugar, and dreams into delightful treats at her family's bakery, "Sofia's Sweets."

Sofia's
SWEETS

One rainy afternoon, while stirring a batch of her special vanilla frosting, something unusual happened. Olli the oven let out a cheerful giggle, and the rolling Pin began to dance across the counter. Startled but curious, Sofia leaned closer.

"What's happening?" she gasped.

7

Welcome, Sofia!" chimed Olli, as his door swung open to reveal a swirl of golden light. "We've been waiting for you! You have discovered the magic of the bakery!"

SOFIA'S SWEETS
Sofia's SWEETS
FLOUR
22 22
SOFIA'S SWEETS
9

With a twinkle in her eye, Sofia watched as the ingredients floated through the air, joining together to create the most beautiful cake she had ever seen. "But how is this possible?" she asked, her heart racing with excitement.

Rosie the rolling Pin chimed in, "In this bakery, every recipe is filled with a sprinkle of magic. Each time you bake with love, we come to life to help you!"

13

Eager to explore, Sofia clapped her hands and suddenly, the flour flew up, creating a gentle cloud that sparkled like stars. The sugar danced in a spiral, and the eggs twirled in delight. Together, they crafted pastries, cookies, and treats that filled the bakery with enchanting aromas.

Sofia's
SWEETS
15

As the days passed, Sofia learned how to use her magic. She discovered that each treat had its own special charm. Chocolate chip cookies made everyone laugh, while French Macarons spread love. Each day, the bakery buzzed with laughter and delight, drawing townsfolk from near and far.

Sofia's
SWEETS

One evening, as the sun set in hues of pink and gold, a worried little boy named Niko entered the bakery.

"What can I get for you?"

"My puppy is sick, and I don't know how to make him feel better," he sniffled.

Sofia's SWEETS
SOFIA
19

Sofia knelt beside him and said, "Let's bake something special!" With a flick of the wrist, Olli and Rosie sprang to life. Together, they whipped up a batch of fluffy dog-friendly cookies, infused with love and a dash of magic.

SOFIA
BAK
Sofia
love
21

As they finished, Sofia handed Niko a heart-shaped bone with the word Love on it. "Give this to your puppy," she said with a smile.

SOFIA'S
SWEETS
23

The next day, Niko returned, his face beaming. "Finn loved it! He's all better now! Thank you, Sofia!" The townsfolk cheered, and the bakery glowed with warmth.

SOFIA'S
SWEETS
25

Sofia realized that the true magic of her bakery wasn't just in the baking—it was in sharing joy and love with others. From that day on, she used her magical bakery to help everyone in Sweetsville, creating not just delicious treats, but also sweet memories that would last a lifetime.

Sofia's
SWEETS

And so, the enchanted bakery continued to bloom, where every sprinkle of flour and dash of sugar carried the magic of friendship, kindness, and love.

Thank You For
Supporting
Sofia's Stories
29

ABOUT THE AUTHOR
By: Francesca Baldino

Francesca Baldino was a pastry chef turned author. She started writing one day after reading to her newborn, Sofia. She took her love of baking and the love for her daughter and put them together to create Sofia and the Magical Bakery. The characters are based on people who have influenced Francesca throughout her life. Sofia's Magical bakery will keep you and your little one wanting to read it again and again! See where Sofia's adventures will take her next!

shero.
Publishing
SHEROPUBLISHING.COM